Wait a Minute, Ruby!

First published 2009
Evans Brothers Limited
2A Portman Mansions
Chiltern Street
London W1U 6NR

British Library Cataloguing in Publication Data

Chapman, Mary.
Wait a minute, Ruby! -- (Spirals)
1. Children's stories.
I. Title II. Series
823.9'2-dc22

ISBN: 978 0 237 53882 8 (hb)
ISBN: 978 0 237 53888 0 (pb)

Printed in China

Editor: Louise John
Design: Robert Walster
Production: Jenny Mulvanny

Wait a Minute, Ruby!

Mary Chapman
and Nick Schon

"Mu-um!" shouted Ruby. "Can you help me to…?"

"Wait a minute, Ruby," said Mum. "Can't you see I'm busy? I'm getting a really strong signal. I'm sure there's something interesting down here."

Ruby sighed a deep sigh, and went back into the house.

"Da-ad," said Ruby. "Can you help me to...?"

"Wait a minute, Ruby," said Dad. "Can't you see I'm busy cooking tea?"

Ruby turned away and plodded up the stairs.

"Gra-an," began Ruby. "Can you help me to...?"

"Wait a minute, Ruby," said Gran. "Can't you see I'm busy? I've just found this amazing website about deep-sea diving."

"Forget it!" said Ruby, and stomped along the landing to her room.

"Nobody has time for me," muttered Ruby. "Not a single person in my *whole* family."

She pulled open a drawer and scooped up knickers, socks and pyjamas. She opened her wardrobe and grabbed T-shirts and jeans. She stuffed them all into her bag. Then she found her favourite book and her favourite teddy bear and squeezed them in, too.

“I’m *not* a nuisance,” she said, “and I’m *not* staying here just to be ignored.”

Ruby sneaked into the bathroom
for her toothbrush and toothpaste.
She popped them into her pocket.

She crept past Gran's room, down the stairs, through the hall...

...into the kitchen (soon her pockets were bulging), and out of the back door.

She went down the garden path and
into the shed...

...and nobody noticed, not Gran, not Dad, not Mum. They were all FAR TOO BUSY!

"I wish I was a famous detective," thought Ruby.

Wait a minute. Can't you see I'm busy solving crimes?

"I wish I was a famous TV chef," thought Ruby.

Wait a minute. Can't you see I'm busy cooking?

"I wish I was a famous explorer," thought Ruby.

Wait a minute. Can't you see I'm busy exploring?

"Anyone seen Ruby?" asked Mum.

"I haven't," said Gran.

"Nor me," said Dad.

"She'll be in her room," said Gran. "I'll get her."

Travel

“She’s not there,” said Gran. “Her bag’s gone, and some clothes, and her teddy!”

“She’s run away!” said Mum. “And it’s getting dark!”

“DON’T PANIC!” shouted Dad.

"I can't remember when I last saw her," said Mum.

"Nor can I," said Dad.

"Nor me," said Gran, "but she can't have gone far."

"Let's look in the garden first," said Mum.

"We must KEEP CALM!" shouted Dad.

"Ruby! Ruby!" they called.

It was getting darker and darker.

"Ruby! Ruby!"

"She's not here," said Mum. "Where on earth is she? We'd better call the police."

"DON'T PANIC!" shouted Dad.

"Look!" said Gran. "There's a light on in the shed."

"Ruby, there you are! We've been so worried," said Mum.

"Come and have your tea," said Gran.

"Spaghetti bolognaise, your favourite," said Dad.

Ruby glanced up from her book.

"Wait a minute, all of you. Can't you see I'm BUSY?"

Why not try reading another **Spirals** book?

Megan's Tick Tock Rocket by Andrew Fusek Peters, Polly Peters
HB: 978 0237 53348 0 PB: 978 0237 53342 7

Growl! by Vivian French
HB: 978 0237 53351 0 PB: 978 0237 53345 8

John and the River Monster by Paul Harrison
HB: 978 0237 53350 2 PB: 978 0237 53344 1

Froggy Went a Hopping by Alan Durant
HB: 978 0237 53352 9 PB: 978 0237 53346 5

Amy's Slippers by Mary Chapman
HB: 978 0237 53353 3 PB: 978 0237 53347 2

The Flamingo Who Forgot by Alan Durant
HB: 978 0237 53349 6 PB: 978 0237 53343 4

Glub! by Penny Little
HB: 978 0237 53462 2 PB: 978 0237 53461 5

The Grumpy Queen by Valerie Wilding
HB: 978 0237 53460 8 PB: 978 0237 53459 2

Happy by Mara Bergman
HB: 978 0237 53532 2 PB: 978 0237 53536 0

Sink or Swim by Dereen Taylor
HB: 978 0237 53531 5 PB: 978 0237 53535 3

Sophie's Timepiece by Mary Chapman
HB: 978 0237 53530 8 PB: 978 0237 53534 6

The Perfect Prince by Paul Harrison
HB: 978 0237 53533 9 PB: 978 0237 53537 7

Tuva by Mick Gowar
HB: 978 0237 53879 8 PB: 978 0237 53885 9

Wait a Minute, Ruby! by Mary Chapman
HB: 978 0237 53882 8 PB: 978 0237 53888 0

George and the Dragonfly by Andy Blackford
HB: 978 0237 53878 1 PB: 978 0237 53884 2

Monster in the Garden by Anne Rooney
HB: 978 0237 53883 5 PB: 978 0237 53889 7

Just Custard by Joe Hackett
HB: 978 0237 53881 1 PB: 978 0237 53887 3

The King of Kites by Judith Heneghan
HB: 978 0237 53880 4 PB: 978 0237 53886 6